To Tyler Nevins and Tracey Keevan

First Edition, May 2017
20 19 18 17 16 15 14 13 12
FAC-039745-21258
This book is set in Century 725/Monotype; Grilled Cheese/Fontbros; Typography of Coop, Fink, Neutraface/House Industries
Printed in South Korea
Reinforced binding

Library of Congress Cataloging-in-Publication Control Number: 2016042481
ISBN 978-1-4847-9967-3

Visit www.hyperionbooksforchildren.com and www.pigeonpresents.com

# An ELEPHANT & PIGGIE BIGGIE!
## Volume 1

An ELEPHANT & PIGGIE Book

Today I Will Fly!

By Mo Willems

Page 3

An ELEPHANT & PIGGIE Book

Watch Me Throw the Ball!

By Mo Willems

Page 65

An ELEPHANT & PIGGIE Book

Can I Play Too?

By Mo Willems

Page 127

Let's Go for a Drive!

By Mo Willems

Page 189

An ELEPHANT & PIGGIE Book

I Really Like Slop!

By Mo Willems

Page 251

## By Mo Willems

Hyperion Books for Children / *New York*

Originally published in April 2007.

# Today I Will Fly!

By **Mo Willems**

An **ELEPHANT & PIGGIE** Book
Hyperion Books for Children / *New York*

You will not fly tomorrow.

Fly, fly, fly, fly, fly

You need help.

I will get help!

Thank you for your help!

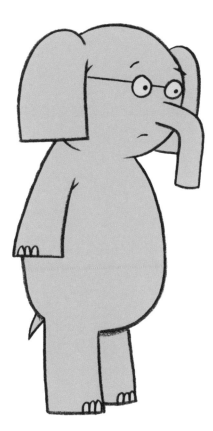

I will eat lunch.

Good-bye!

Fly! Fly! Fly!

You need help.

I do need help.

Will you help me?

I will.
I will help you.

Thank you.

Hello!

You . . . you are FLYING!

You are flying today!

I am *not* flying!

I am getting help.

Thank you for your help!

Tomorrow *I* will fly!

Good luck.

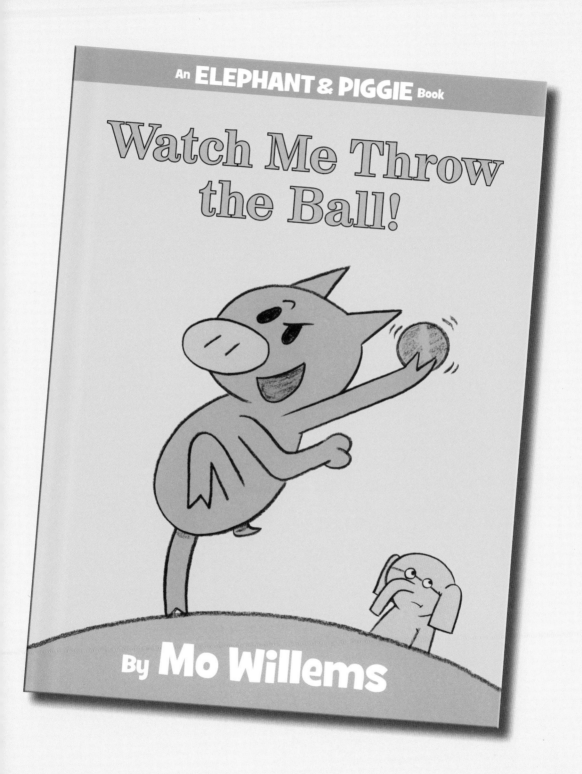

Originally published in March 2009.

# Watch Me Throw the Ball!

By **Mo Willems**

An **ELEPHANT & PIGGIE** Book

Hyperion Books for Children / *New York*

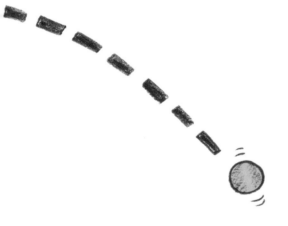

A ball!

This is
your ball?

I am very good
at throwing.

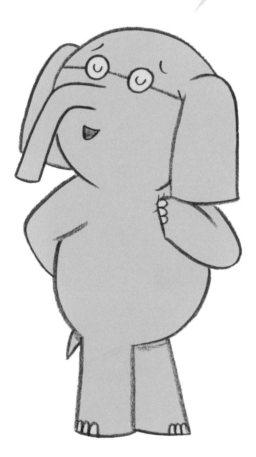

May I throw
your ball?

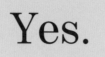

# THE PIG IS

FLING!

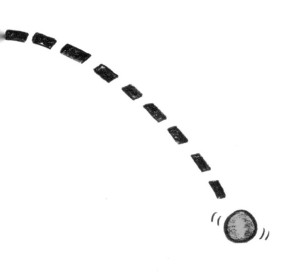

PLOP!

95

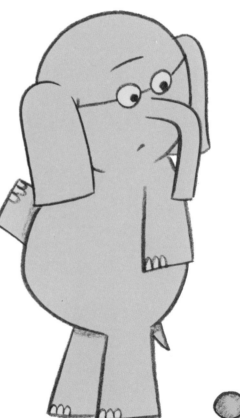

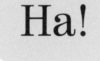

The ball flew behind you and fell here!

You are right, Gerald.
I did not really throw
the ball very far.

FLING!

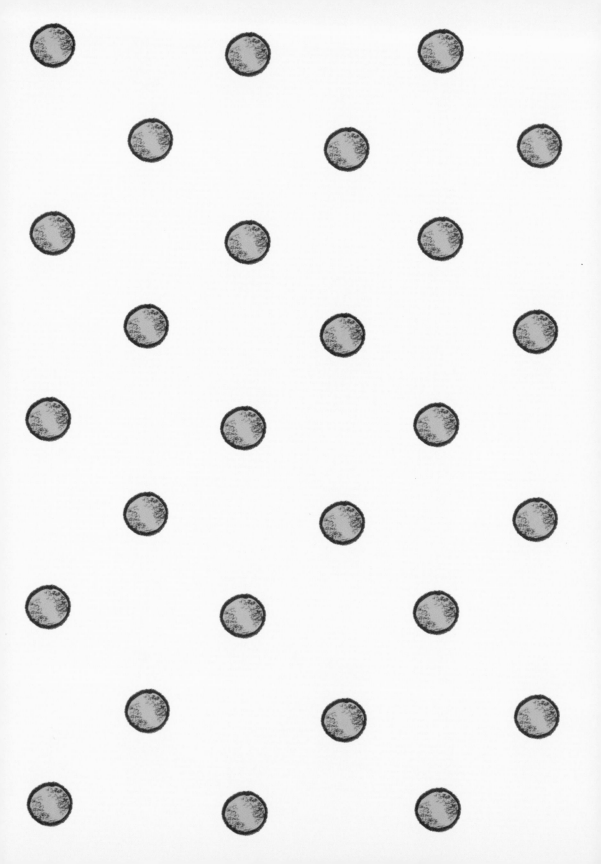

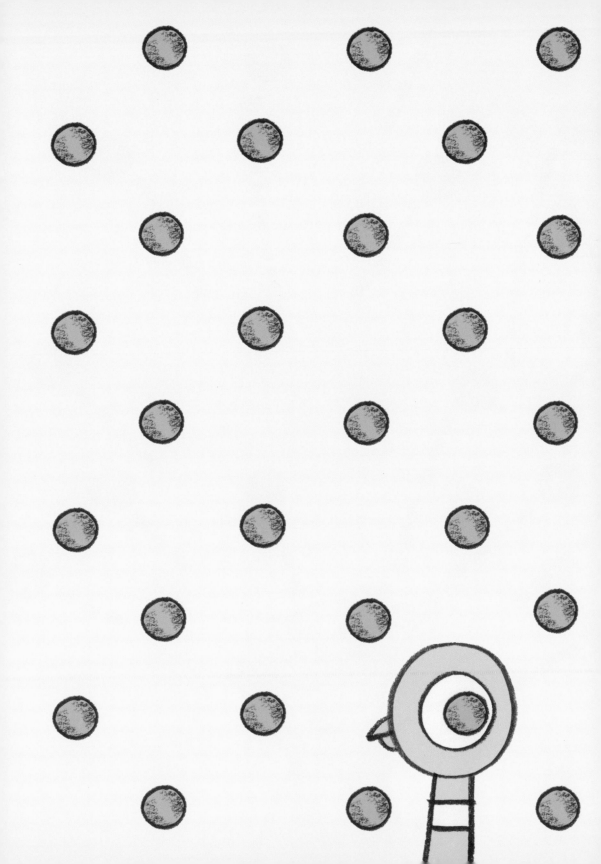

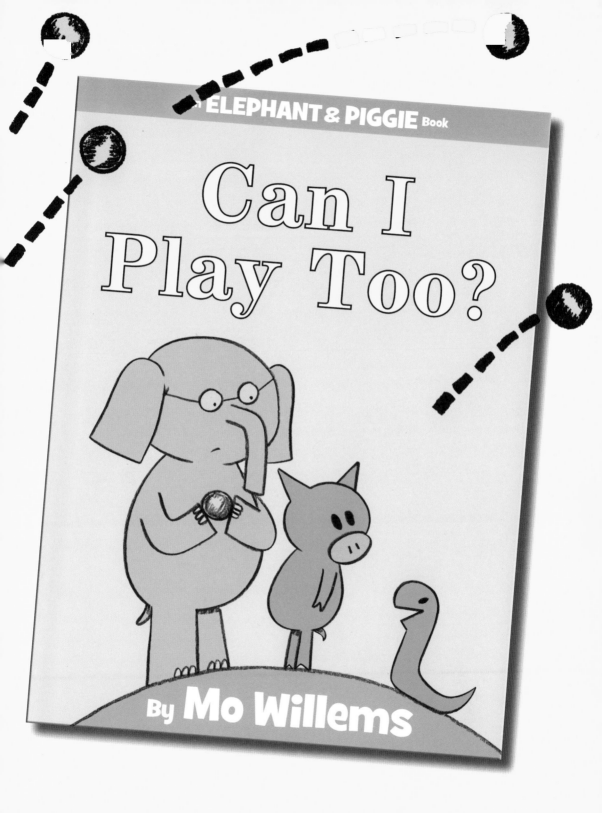

# Can I Play Too?

By Mo Willems

An ELEPHANT & PIGGIE Book

Hyperion Books for Children / *New York*

Piggie!

Let's play catch!

I love playing catch with friends!

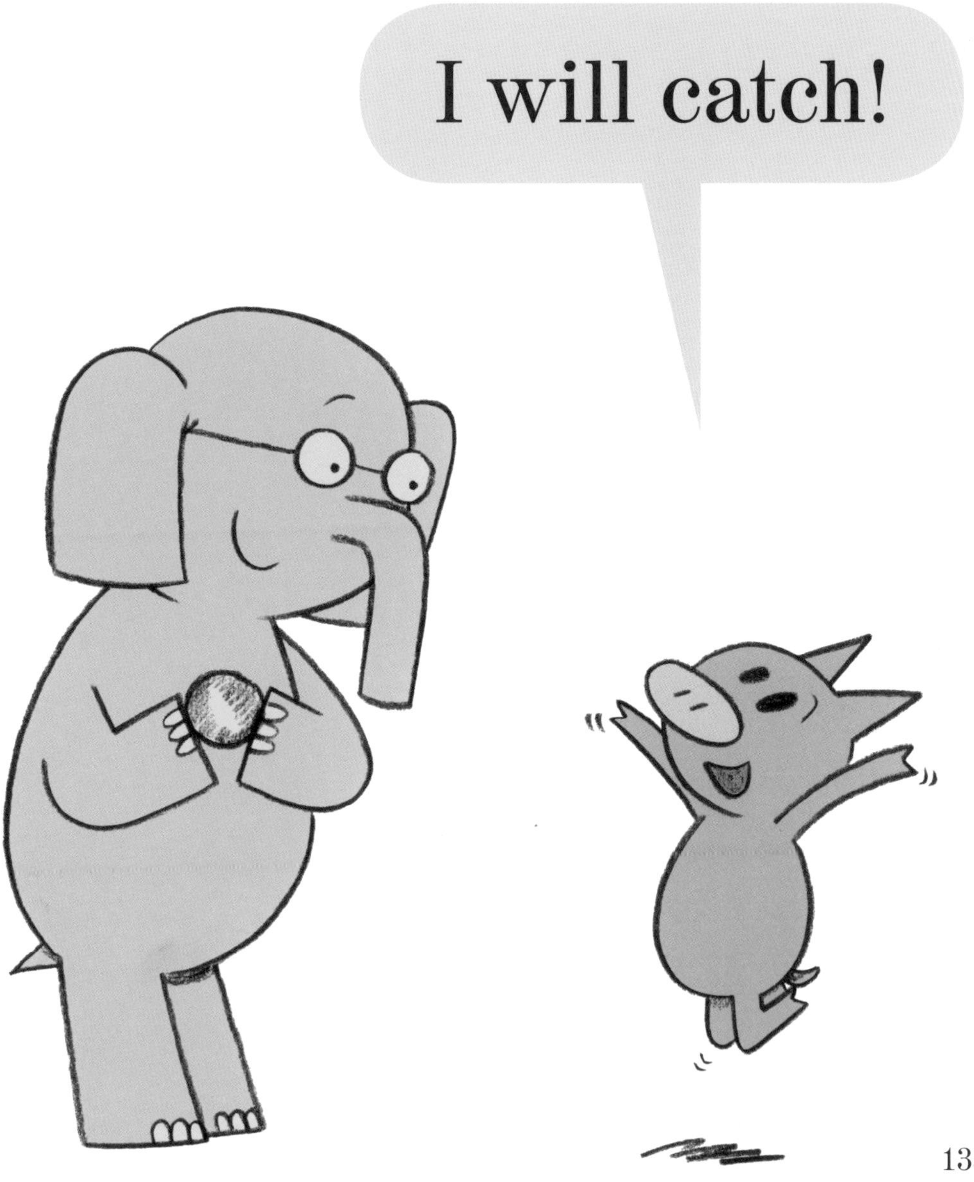
I will catch!

Excuse me!

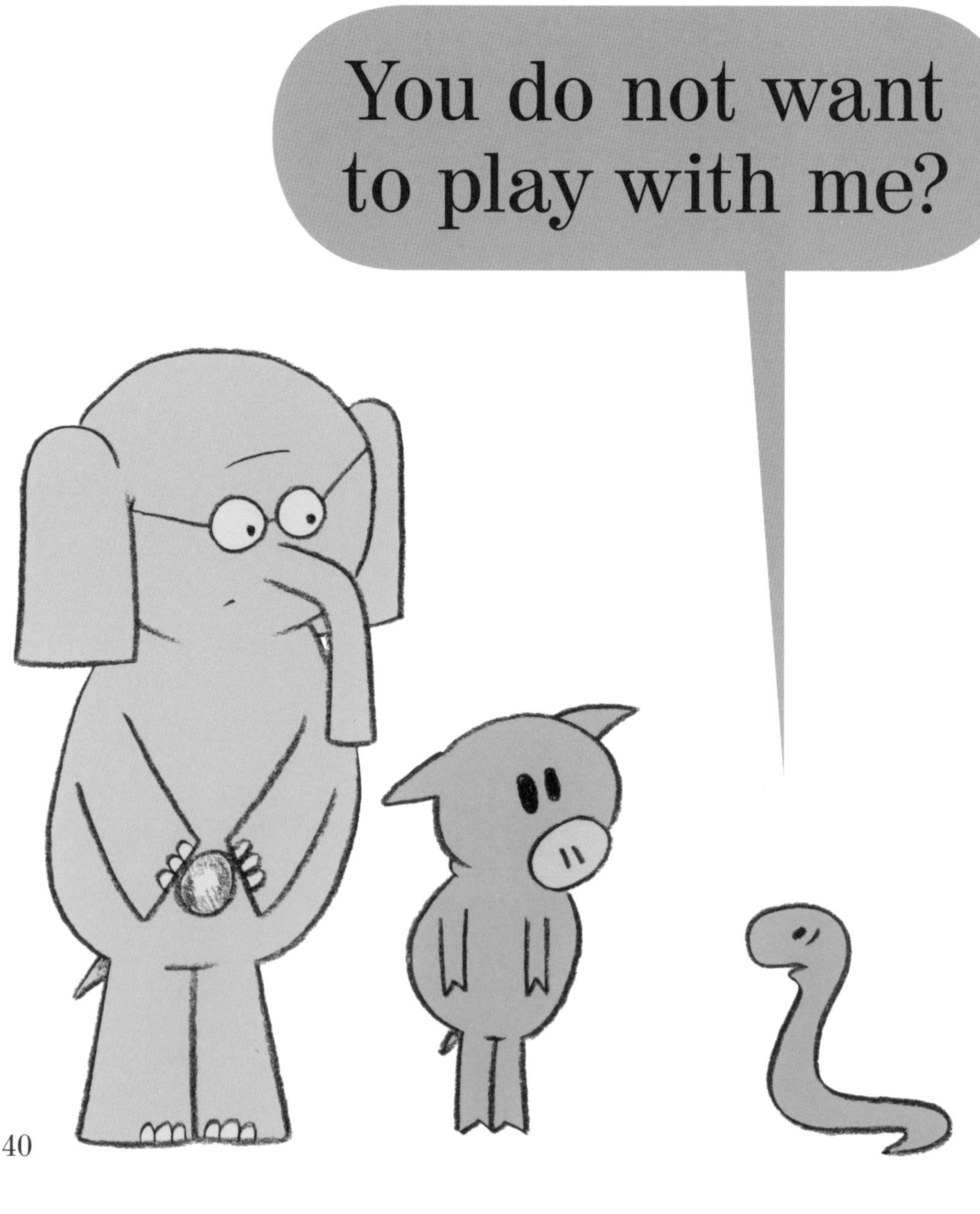
You do not want to play with me?

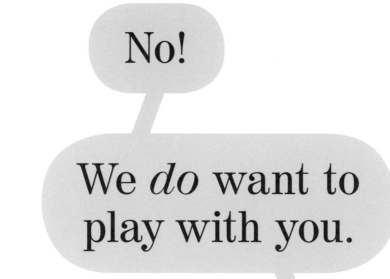

We are
playing
catch.

145

Hee-hee!
*Ha-ha!*
Hee-hee!
*Ha-ha!*
Hee-hee!

158

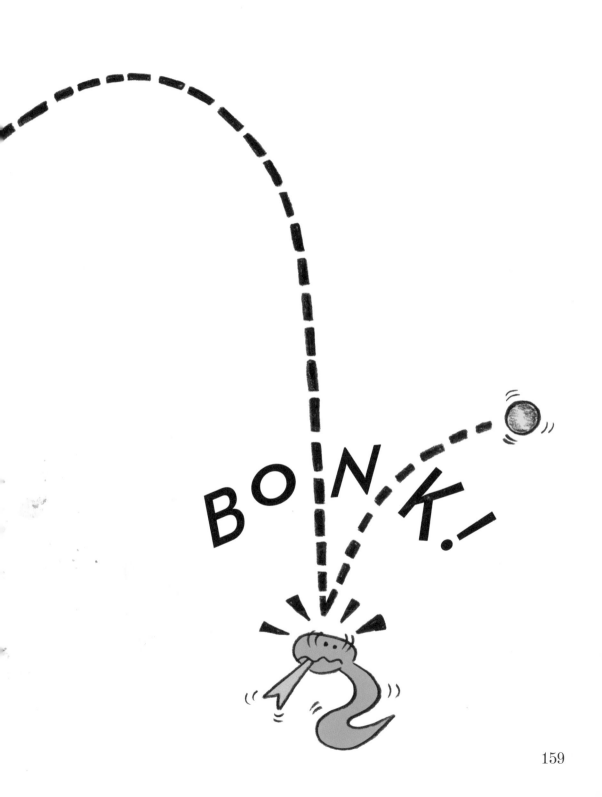

BONK!

161

BONK!

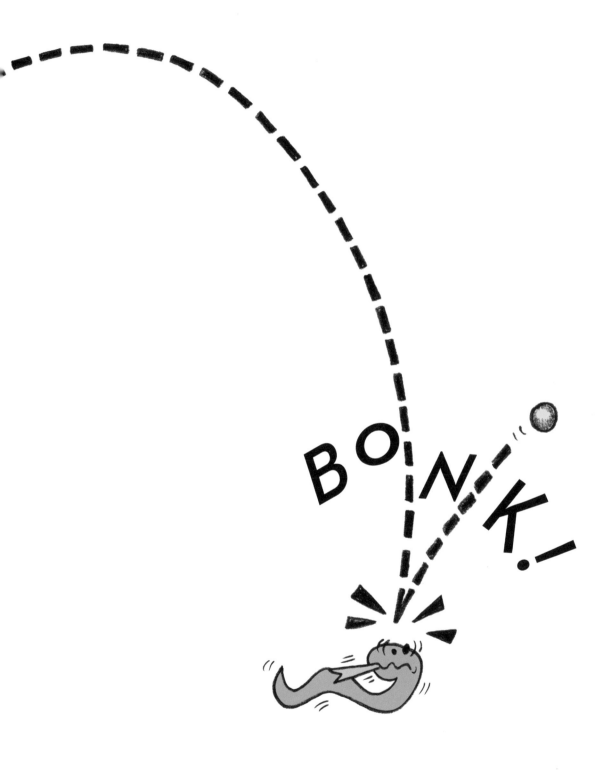

BONK!

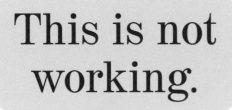

This is not working.

We need a new idea.....

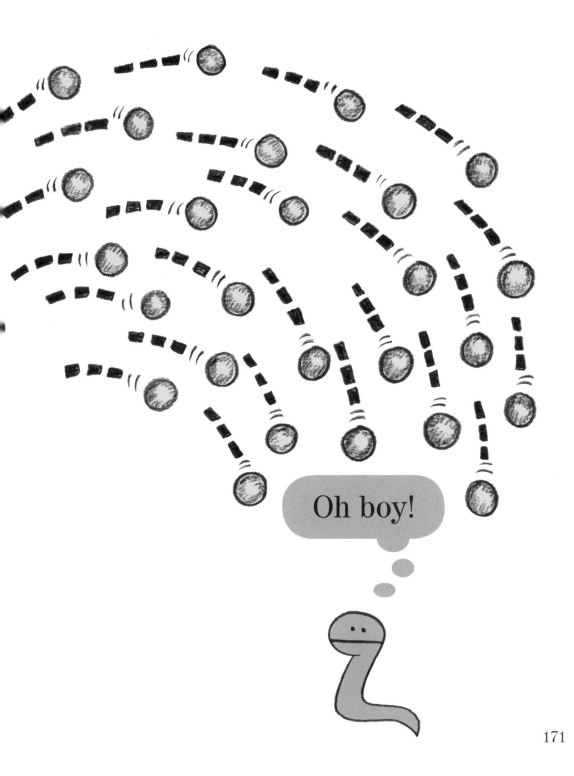

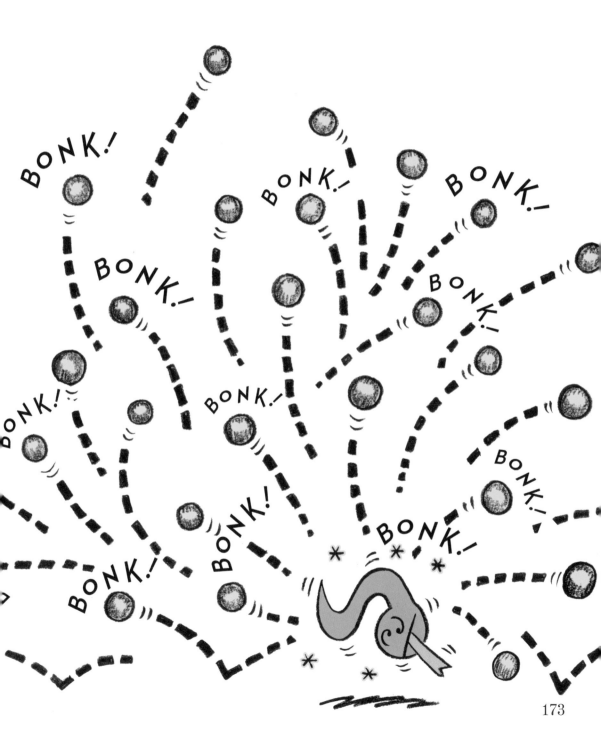

173

174

179

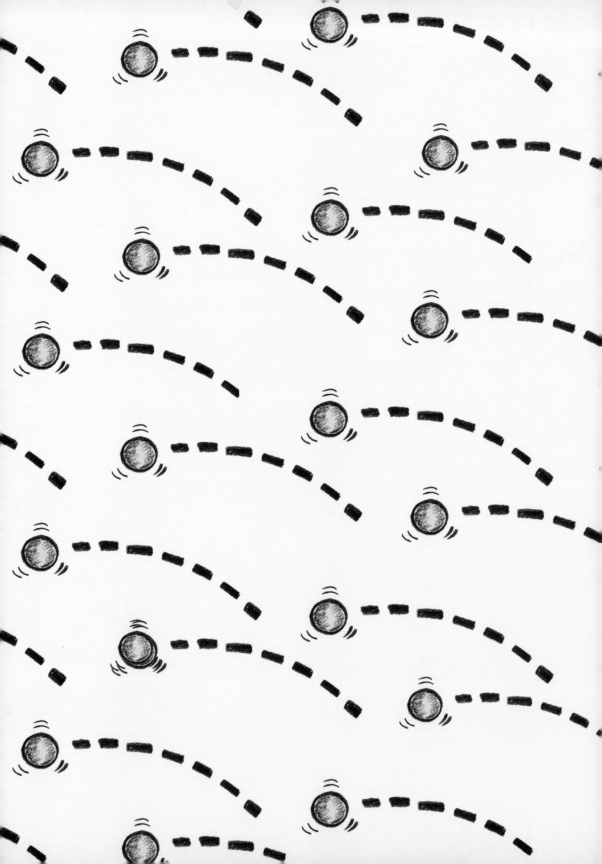

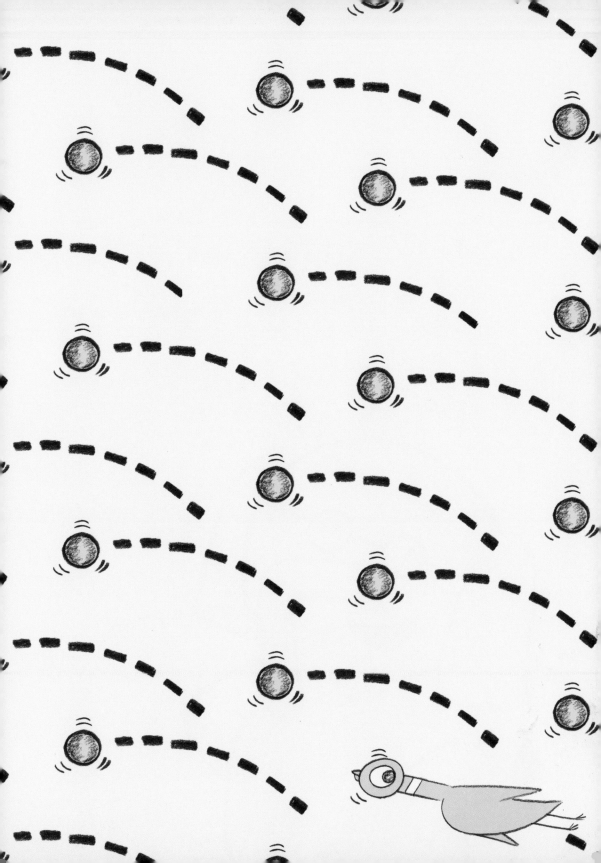

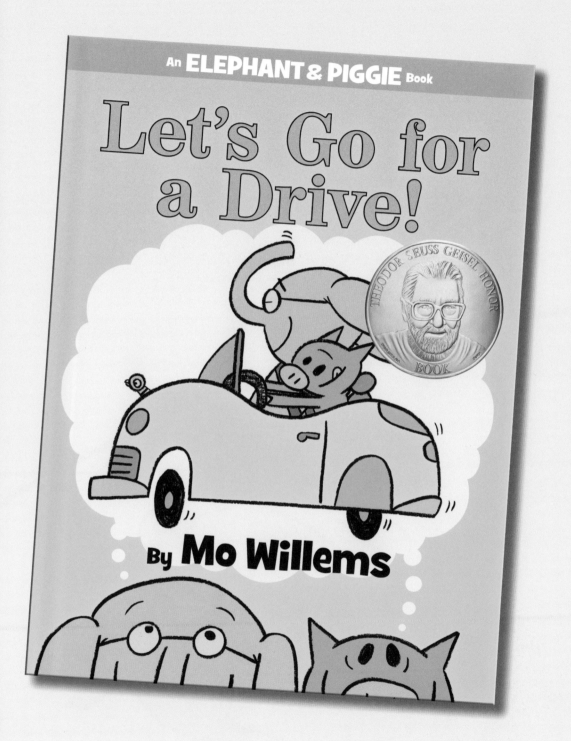

Originally published in October 2012.

# Let's Go for a Drive!

An **ELEPHANT & PIGGIE** Book

Hyperion Books for Children / *New York*

By Mo Willems

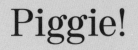

Piggie!

I have a great idea!

195

First, we need
a map.

I have
a map!

Bringing sunglasses on a drive is smart planning.

Make a plan and stick to it, is what I say.

218

225

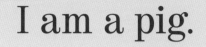

244

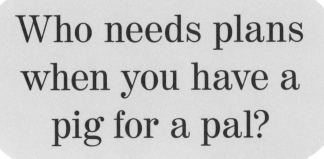

Originally published in October 2015.

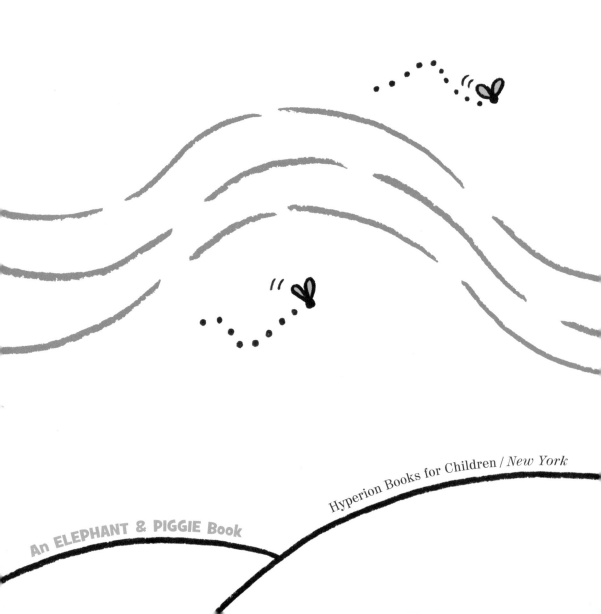

An ELEPHANT & PIGGIE Book

Hyperion Books for Children / *New York*

POP!

WALK    WALK    WALK    WALK

WALK

Piggie.

Yes, Gerald?

287

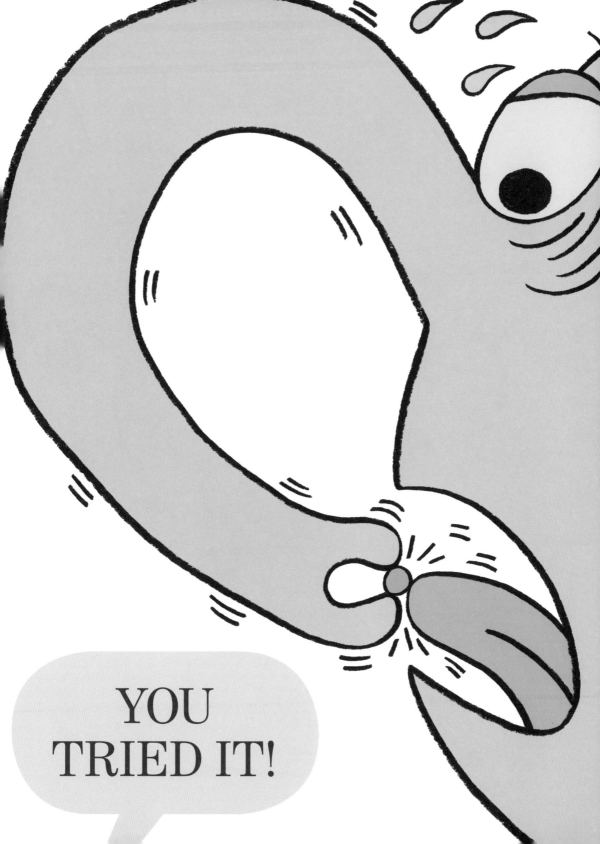

299

# Dear Reader,

# Wow!

You read five Elephant & Piggie adventures in one book! Congratulations!

Reading every day makes you a better reader, just like drawing every day makes you a better draw-er!

When I was a kid, I would practice drawing Charlie Brown and Snoopy. Sometimes it's fun to draw characters you know, but in your own style. My friend Dan Santat drew his own versions of Elephant and Piggie. I love it!

What do your Elephant and Piggie look like?

Your pal,

Mo!